Auth

P9-AOP-759

12051

TEN FURRY MONSTERS
To librarians, parents, and teachers:

Ten Furry Monsters is a Parents Magazine READ ALOUD Original — one title in a series of colorfully illustrated and fun-to-read stories that young readers will be sure to come back to time and time again.

Now, in this special school and library edition of *Ten Furry Monsters,* adults have an even greater opportunity to increase children's responsiveness to reading and learning — and to have fun every step of the way.

When you finish this story, check the special section at the back of the book. There you will find games, projects, things to talk about, and other educational activities designed to make reading enjoyable by giving children and adults a chance to play together, work together, and talk over the story they have just read.

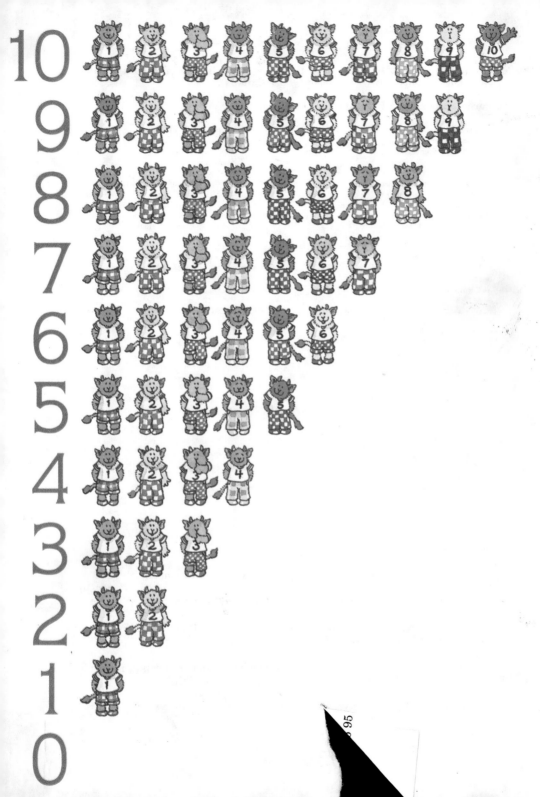

For a free color catalog describing Gareth Stevens' list of high-quality books, call 1-800-341-3569 (USA) or 1-800-461-9120 (Canada).

Parents Magazine READ ALOUD Originals:

Golly Gump Swallowed a Fly
The Housekeeper's Dog
Who Put the Pepper in the Pot?
Those Terrible Toy-Breakers
The Ghost in Dobbs Diner
The Biggest Shadow in the Zoo
The Old Man and the Afternoon Cat
Septimus Bean and His Amazing Machine
Sherlock Chick's First Case
A Garden for Miss Mouse
Witches Four
Bread and Honey
Pigs in the House
Milk and Cookies
But No Elephants
No Carrots for Harry!
Snow Lion
Henry's Awful Mistake
The Fox with Cold Feet
Get Well, Clown-Arounds!
Pets I Wouldn't Pick
Sherlock Chick and the Giant
  Egg Mystery
Cats! Cats! Cats!

Henry's Important Date
Elephant Goes to School
Rabbit's New Rug
Sand Cake
Socks for Supper
The Clown-Arounds Go on Vacation
The Little Witch Sisters
The Very Bumpy Bus Ride
Henry Babysits
There's No Place Like Home
Up Goes Mr. Downs
Bicycle Bear
Sweet Dreams, Clown-Arounds!
The Man Who Cooked for Himself
Where's Rufus?
The Giggle Book
Pickle Things
Oh, So Silly!
The Peace-and-Quiet Diner
Ten Furry Monsters
One Little Monkey
The Silly Tail Book
Aren't You Forgetting Something, Fiona?

ISBN 0-8368-0989-0

This North American library edition published in 1994 by Gareth Stevens Publishing, 1555 North RiverCenter Drive, Suite 201, Milwaukee, Wisconsin 53212, USA, under an arrangement with Parents Magazine Press, New York.

Text © 1984 by Stephanie Calmenson. Illustrations © 1984 by Maxie Chambliss. End matter © 1994 by Gareth Stevens, Inc.

Printed in the United States of America

1 2 3 4 5 6 7 8 9 99 98 97 96 95 94

Ten Furry
Monsters

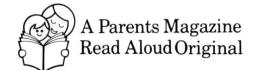

A Parents Magazine
Read Aloud Original

Ten Furry Monsters

by Stephanie Calmenson
pictures by Maxie Chambliss

Parents Magazine Press • New York

Gareth Stevens Publishing • Milwaukee

To my brother, Michael—*S.C.*

From Number Five
to Numbers Three and Four—*M.C.*

Ten furry monsters,
Having monster fun,

Hear their mother calling,
And gather one by one.

"I'm off to buy our lunch now.
I must be on my way.
No one is to wander off.
This is where you stay.

Do not leave the park.
Don't go far to play.
Remember, all my monsters,
This is where you stay."

Ten furry monsters,

Sitting in a line...

One went to hide;
Now there are nine.

Nine furry monsters
Were told that they must wait...

But another went away;
Now there are just eight.

Eight furry monsters,
Up to their old tricks...

Two disappeared;
Now there are six.

Six furry monsters
Really should have tried...

To stay where they were told;
Now there are just five!

Five furry monsters,
Listen to them snore...

One woke up and slipped away;
Now there are just four.

Four furry monsters,
Still where they should be...

Did one forget what mother said?
Now there are just three.

Three furry monsters
Hear an owl call, "Whoo"...

One ran to find it;
Now there are two.

Two furry monsters,
Playing in the sun...

One got up to look for shade;
Now there is just one.

One furry monster
Wants to join the fun...

31

He goes off with all the rest;
Now there are none...

No furry monsters,
And mother's back again.
"I know you're all here somewhere,
So I will count to ten."

"One, two, three..."

"Four, five, six..."

"Seven, eight, nine..."

"Ten!"

Ten furry monsters
Were not gone for long...

Mother's glad to see them,

Back where they belong!

Notes to Grown-ups

Major Themes
Here is a quick guide to the significant themes and concepts at work in *Ten Furry Monsters:*

- Counting can be fun: as young readers will find out by keeping track of the little monsters in the park.
- Family activities: the monster family plays together and shares affection and joy in being together.
- Counting and rhyming: both are orderly and both help children learn conceptual thinking.

Step-by-step Ideas for Reading and Talking
Here are some ideas for further give-and-take between grown-ups and children. The following topics encourage creative discussion of *Ten Furry Monsters* and invite the kind of open-ended response that is consistent with many contemporary approaches to reading, including Whole Language:

- Learning to follow directions is a necessary skill for young people to learn. In the case of the little monsters, why is it so important for them to listen to their mother's directions? Were they being naughty or were they really doing what she asked them to do? What are some other examples that show how listening to someone who cares about you is important?
- The little monsters not only play well together, they also enjoy being with each other. What are some of the games the monsters play? What types of playground equipment do they choose to play on? What toys do they play with? Can you tell if the monsters share their belongings with each other? How can you tell the monsters have affection for each other?

Games for Learning

Games and activities can stimulate young readers and listeners alike to find out more about words, numbers, and ideas. Here's one idea for turning learning into fun:

Monster Math

These friendly little monsters are just waiting to teach your child the basics of subtraction. Long before a child learns the addition and subtraction tables, she or he needs to understand what happens to quantities of things when you add one more or take one away. To develop this concept, read the story together again, but this time help your child reenact the subtraction process by starting with ten objects (checkers, cereal pieces, beans, spoons, or whatever you have ten of) and taking one away each time one furry little monster disappears in the story. Then add them back again as the monsters return to their mother.

About the Author

STEPHANIE CALMENSON says that, just like the monsters in her book, she and her brother found lots of ways to have fun without breaking any rules. "We weren't allowed to play ball in the house, but we invented a great indoor game of basketball using rolled-up socks for a ball and a bent wire hanger attached to a closet door for a hoop."

Ms. Calmenson is the author of many popular books for children. Before turning to writing full-time, she was an elementary school teacher and a children's book editor. Ms. Calmenson lives in New York City.

About the Artist

MAXIE CHAMBLISS grew up in a large family in New Jersey. "With so many [children] running around," she explains, "my dad decided to number us just to keep track. I've been Number Five ever since. It made sense to me that any smart monster mother would have done the same thing."

0

1

2

3

4

5

6

7

8

9

10

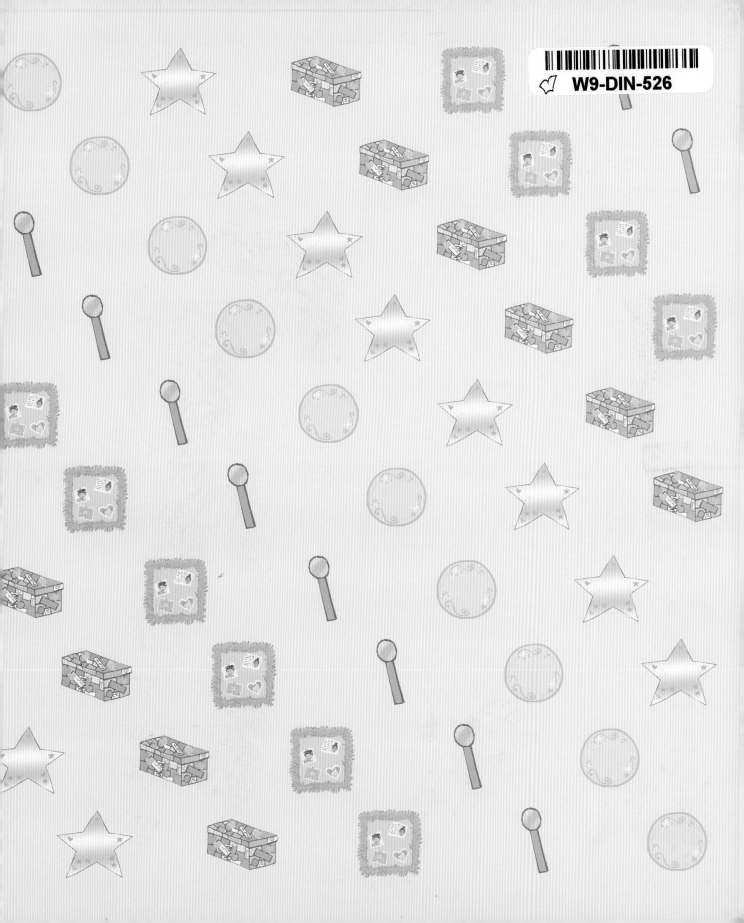

Note: All activities in this book should be performed with
adult supervision. Common sense and care are essential to the
conduct of any and all activities, whether described in this book or not.
Neither the author nor the publisher assumes any responsibility
for any injuries or damages arising from any activities.

KINGFISHER
a Houghton Mifflin Company imprint
222 Berkeley Street
Boston, Massachusetts 02116
www.houghtonmifflinbooks.com

First published in 2006
2 4 6 8 10 9 7 5 3 1

Text copyright © Kingfisher 2006
Illustrations copyright © Jessie Eckel 2006
Created and produced by The Complete Works
St. Mary's Road, Royal Leamington Spa, Warwickshire, CV31 1JP U.K.

LIBRARY OF CONGRESS CATALOGING-IN-PUBLICATION DATA has been applied for.

ISBN 0-7534-5956-6
ISBN 978-07534-5956-0

Printed in China
1TR/0106/SNPLEX/MA(MA)/157MA/F

How to be a Star

in 7 days or less

Illustrated by Jessie Eckel
Written by Lesley Rees

KINGFISHER

BOSTON

Calling All Starlets!

Hi, I'm Danielle, and I want to be a star! I've got a dream, and I'm going to make it come true. Would you like to have star quality—you know, that special something that makes you stand out from all the other wannabes? Well, let me and my friends show you how to get it. And in just seven days you'll be ready to perform in your very own talent show!

Meet my friends Kelly and Scarlett. We're the Rising Stars!

I love to sing.

Kelly was
born to dance.

Scarlett is the actress.

Whatever your talent is, we'll show you how to make the most of it!

We're going to show you how you can be a
true star. You're going to need fabulous hair and
cool clothes. So there's going to be a superstar
makeover and exercises, too. But remember,
starlets, you may have talent, but being a
star takes commitment, determination, practice,
and lots and lots of dedication. Do *you* have
what it takes? If so, let's get started!

Do-Re-Mi!

I love to sing. It's fun, it's easy, and it's something you can do anytime.
Just take a deep breath and go for it—you can be a singing star like me! Did
you know that successful singers think of their voices as instruments?
They have to take care of their voices and exercise them every day.
So here are a few tips to help you care for your "instrument."

The correct posture is important, so:

DO

★ Stand upright
with your back
and neck *straight.*
★ Keep your
knees *loose.*
★ *Relax* your
shoulders.
★ *Smile.*

DON'T

★ Suck in your
stomach.
★ Stretch out
your *neck* like
a turkey.
★ Forget to
breathe.

Got that? Good. Now try this: Hold your arms loosely
by your sides and breathe in slowly. Now sing one
note such as "*do.*" Try to hold it without making the
note shake or running out of breath. You'll get the
hang of it. Try practicing with sounds like "*ooh*" and
"*aah*"—you'll need to use a different mouth shape.

Try going up a scale—*Do, re, mi, fa, so, la, ti, do.*
Try it backward—*Do, ti, la, so, fa, mi, re, do.*

Laaaaaaaaaaaa!

Danielle's Dynamite Doorplate

What does every star need? That's right, a Star Dressing Room. Okay, it's my bedroom, but it's also a great place to practice and plan my glittering career. And what do all stars have on their dressing-room doors? That's right—their names. I made my own doorplate—star-shaped, of course! Follow my easy instructions, and you can have one too.

First of all, take . . .

- ★ star stencil
- ★ mirror board
- ★ scissors
- ★ a pencil
- ★ stickers
- ★ glue and glitter

What you do next . . .

1. Place the star stencil onto the mirror board and trace around it using the pencil.
2. Cut out the star shape. You may need an adult to help you do this.
3. Decorate it with pretty stickers.

4. In the center write your name in fancy lettering with glue, like this:

MISS
(your name)'s
DRESSING ROOM

5. Sprinkle the glue with colored glitter, shake off the excess, and leave it to dry.

Now stick it on your dressing-room door!

Singsong Star

Once you've got the hang of singing, the important thing is to practice as much as possible. Remember, practice makes perfect! But you have to pick a good place to practice if you don't want everyone to hear your mistakes!

Here are a few of my favorite places to practice:

The bathroom

Singing in the shower is fantastic—the tiles really make your voice echo.

Remember my name. Fame!

In front of the mirror

This is a cool place to practice your moves while you sing. I get Kelly to teach me dance routines, or I just make up my own. It can be hard to sing and dance at the same time—but keep trying!

Everywhere!

I love listening to music with my headphones. I can sing along at the same time. My brother goes crazy when I sing in the car, but I ignore him!

Make a Mega Microphone

It's so easy to make your own microphone.

It's a great prop, and it's what every starlet needs.

First of all, take . . .

- ★ some newspaper
- ★ cardboard tube from a roll of paper towels
- ★ tape
- ★ tinfoil
- ★ a paintbrush
- ★ glue
- ★ glitter
- ★ paint

What you do next . . .

1. Roll up the newspaper into a ball—around the size of a tennis ball.
2. Next, paint the cardboard tube your favourite color—mine's hot pink!
3. Cover the newspaper ball with tinfoil.
4. Paint the ball with glue.
5. Now sprinkle it with glitter and leave it to dry.
6. Place the ball on top of the cardboard tube and secure it with tape.
7. Now start singing!

All the World's a Stage . . .

Hi, I'm Scarlett, and I really want to be an actress.
I just love putting on a costume and becoming someone else.
You see, I can be anyone I want to be when I'm on stage—
from a servant to a princess.

As an actress, you'll need to be able to show every type of emotion. So, come on, let's start practicing!

You know how whatever you're feeling shows on your face? Well, I make faces all the time in front of my mirror. It's great practice for an aspiring actress. See if you can look . . .

happy

sad

angry

excited

tired

And no giggling! Try to really *feel* these emotions.

Of course, a great way to begin acting is by playing a simple game like charades. Just think of the title of a movie, a book, or even a song, and then act it out. See if your friends can guess the answer just by watching your body and facial expressions—you can't speak, though, so no cheating! Then swap and see if you can guess what their title is.

Romeo, Romeo! Wherefore art thou, Romeo?

Actresses need to remember their lines, their moves, and to stay in character. Try learning your favorite poem by heart—it's always handy when you are called on to perform at a moment's notice!

Actresses should be able to do different accents. So listen to people from other places and try to imitate them. You can even dress up like them!

What's My Motivation?

As an actress, I can pretend to be anyone or anything. But it can be hard to get into character—imagine me pretending to be a little old lady! Sometimes you need a little extra help to convince yourself, as well as the audience!

It's easier to get into character if you're wearing the right costume. I have a big box in my bedroom that's full of old clothes. I'm always dressing up with my friends to act out scenes from our favorite movies.

This doesn't mean that you have to buy special outfits. I always look out for things that I can add to my collection, so don't let your mom or grandma throw anything away—including your dad and your grandpa's old clothes!

I don't know what she's looking for, but I'm sure it's in there somewhere!

Even scarves, jewelry, hats, and belts that aren't in fashion anymore could be just what you need for the finishing touch on a costume, so save *everything!*

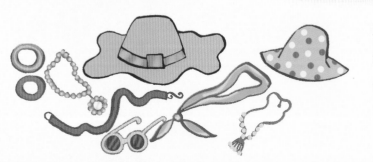

Wonderful Wigs

Sometimes actors wear makeup and a wig to change their appearance. Making wigs is a lot of fun, and it's easy to do. Here's how to make your own—you can make it any color you want to.

First of all, take . . .

★ a swimming cap

★ a black marker

★ scissors

★ yarn of any color cut into long or short pieces

★ a large plastic knitting needle

What you do next . . .

1. Put on the swimming cap and tuck your own hair into it.

2. Use the marker to draw the shape of your hairline around your forehead.

3. Take off the cap and cut along the line so that it's the right shape for your head. You may need an adult to do this part. You don't want to be able to see the cap when the wig is done.

4. Thread the needle with a piece of yarn and push it through the swimming cap.

5. Knot the yarn on the inside of the cap so that the yarn pokes through, like hair.

6. Repeat steps 4 and 5, adding the yarn in rows, until the whole cap is covered. Don't forget to use shorter pieces if you want your wig to have bangs.

Try it on and be amazed by how different you look!

I've always wanted to be blonde!

Remember, you can make lots of different wigs. You can braid the yarn to make dreadlocks or make one with a ridge of spiky hair in the middle, like a punk.

You're a Dancing Queen

Hi, I'm Kelly, and I like to dance. Disco, tap, ballet—I love them all.
I started learning when I was a little girl. Don't worry if
you didn't—it's never too late to start. Dancing is so much fun and is
a great way to stay active and healthy.

Disco dancing is my favorite.
When I'm at a disco, I
sparkle and shimmer in
my coolest clothes.

I don't follow any set moves.
I just feel the rhythm and
move my body in time to
the music—go, girls!

Disco fever!

I'm in the mood for dancing . . .

I've got rhythm . . .

Tap dancing is also a lot of fun. Tap shoes
have special metal pieces on the soles to
make that unique *tap-tap-tapping* sound.
I love practicing in my bedroom, but
my mom isn't so thrilled!

Kelly's Super-Easy Leg Warmers

I love doing ballet in my pink leotard, pretty pink tutu, and dainty ballet shoes. It's given me lots of confidence and has improved my balance and coordination. In my ballet class I start by putting on my leg warmers and doing some stretches so that my muscles are warmed up. Let me show you how to make a pair.

First of all, take . . .

★ an old pair of long socks

★ scissors

★ a needle and thread

What you do next . . .

1. Take the old pair of long socks and cut off the feet.
2. Then fold over the ends, making a hem, and sew them down so that they don't fray. You might need an adult to help with this.

3. Pull them on and "scrunch" them down to create the right effect.

Now—scrrrunch!

The next fashion protégée!

Voilà! Your very own leg warmers.

Grace and poise

Don't Stop the Music!

One thing you really need to do before you start
dancing is warm up and S-T-R-E-T-C-H those muscles.
It's important to do this—otherwise you could hurt yourself.
Here are a few simple exercises that I always do, just to get you started.

March or jog on the spot. Come on, girls—
get those knees up!

Keep your legs straight and together. Now bend
forward and see if you can touch the floor.
Gently stretch as far as you can—but don't
push too hard. Stop if it starts to hurt.

*Streeeeeetch,
but don't overdo it*

Stand or sit and put your arms above your head
and then stretch. Slowly bend over to the side from
your waist. Move back to the middle, and then
bend to the other side.

Stand with your back to the wall and gently
slide downward, slowly bending your knees.
Now hold it there. Then gently slide back up
to a standing position.

Remember, do the exercises gently and don't strain your muscles.

Practice every day, and soon you'll become really flexible!

Kelly's CD Box

When I'm exercising, I *have* to do it along to music. It's so much more fun. But I ended up with so many CDs that I needed somewhere to keep them (to stop my mom from yelling about the mess!). So I made a cool CD box. If you'd like one too, just follow my instructions.

First of all, take . . .

★ scissors   ★ glue
★ glossy magazines   ★ stickers
★ an old shoe box

What you do next . . .

1. Carefully cut out pictures of your favorite stars and other cool pictures from magazines.
2. Take your shoe box and glue the pictures all over the outside, inside, and lid. Overlap them for a cool effect.

3. Cut out fun words like "Cool!," "Fabulous!," and "Wow!" and stick these on too.
4. Paint glue over the whole box to protect the pictures, and then leave it to dry.
5. Add glittery stickers.
6. Fill the box with CDs.

Result—one neat room, and one happy mom!

Now I have space to dance!

Who's Your Inspiration?

Now, girls, a good way to get yourself on the road to stardom is to do some simple research. Who's your favorite singer, actor, or dancer? What gives them the "WOW!" factor? Could you achieve it too?

Picture-Perfect Tackboard

Tackboards are a great way to display info about your favorite star. We made our own, and you can too—it's easy!

First of all, take . . .

★ paint and a paintbrush

★ two cork floor tiles

★ glue

★ a stapler

★ ribbon or fake fur trim

★ thumbtacks

★ old magazines

What you do next . . .

1. Paint one tile your favorite color and leave it to dry.

2. Glue the tiles together, with the painted side facing out.

3. Glue or staple some funky ribbon or fake fur around the edge of the tile. I used hot pink!

4. Now cut out pictures of your favorite stars, clothes, or hairdos and pin them onto your board.

5. Add phrases like "You're a star!" or "Think big!" to inspire you.

6. Now stick the tackboard to your bedroom wall and study it!

Magazines, movies, and TV are all great places to study the stars. Look carefully. Can you see what they have that makes them stand out from the crowd? Try making a list of what you like best about your favorite star—you know, hair, clothes, and makeup. Now practice getting that look for yourself.

I've SO got what it takes!

Even stars need to look where they're going!

Remember that being a star isn't just about performing—you have to behave like a star at all times. That doesn't mean that you should be a demanding diva, by the way. Real stars should always be nice to people and think of others first. Try to remember that when you are a megastar!

Looking the Part

Okay, starlets—if you're going to be a star, you have to look the part. Personal appearance is VERY important, so spend some time perfecting your look. You've studied your favorite stars to see how they do it. Now see if you can do it too.

So, let's start with the basics. First, make sure your skin is in good condition. To get that healthy glow, you need to cleanse inside and out. So eat lots of fresh fruits and vegetables (yes, even the green stuff!), drink lots of water, and make sure your skin is squeaky-clean by using a facial cleanser that is suitable for your skin type.

For beautiful skin— eat beautiful broccoli!

Now it's time to talk about makeup. Practice applying eye shadow and lip gloss until you get the look you want. Don't worry if you don't get it right at first—just wash it off and start again. You and your friends can practice on each other. Body glitter can be applied along your cheekbones and shoulders to catch the light as you sparkle on stage. And stick-on jewels are perfect for that "diva" look.

You can make curls by twisting wet hair, clipping it into place, and drying it with a blow-dryer.

Add jeweled clips for glamour, if you like.

Try out different styles so that you can change your image whenever you want.

You look fabulous! Just like a true star. But make sure that your clothes are right for the occasion— I mean, can you really wear a long, glittery dress to school? Have lots of accessories—bags, belts, hats, scarves, and jewelry. They can transform any outfit from ordinary to "wow"! And don't forget your sunglasses. Stars wear these all the time. When you're inside, you can still wear them—just slide them on top of your head. How cool are you?

Calling All Stars!

Your show is only one day away. You're working hard and practicing your routines, but don't forget your audience—they're important too! So start publicizing—after all, you don't want anyone to miss seeing tomorrow's stars, do you?

Put Up Posters

First, put up tons of posters, telling everyone the three Ws: what, where, and when. It's so easy—take a sheet of plain paper and write something like this:

Use the stickers provided to decorate it and make it as bright and sparkly as you can with bold colors and glitter. Stick up the posters where your target audience will see them—in the kitchen . . .

COME AND SEE
A TALENT SHOW
by
THE RISING STARS
(put the name of your group)
at
THE STAR ACADEMY
(put where you're having it)
on
(put the date)
at
(put the time)

. . . or even in the bathroom!

What's in a Name?

You've publicized your show—but how about publicizing yourself? Why not wear fun pins telling everyone that you're a Rising Star? They're so simple!

First of all, take . . .

- ★ an empty cereal box
- ★ scissors
- ★ pencils or colored pens
- ★ a cup
- ★ glue pen
- ★ glitter
- ★ safety pins
- ★ tape

What you do next . . .

1. Carefully cut the front and back off the cereal box.
2. Put the cup upside down on top of the cut-out cardboard. Trace around the cup's rim, and then carefully cut this out.

3. Write something like "Trainee star!," "Gonna be BIG!," or "Remember my name!" and add swirls and stars.
4. Go over everything with a glue pen. Sprinkle glitter on it, and then tip off the excess and wait for it to dry.

5. Place a safety pin on the back and secure it with tape.

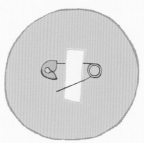

Why not use the stencils that came with this book and make some star- or heart-shaped pins? Make one for your parents or grandparents—it could say "Star's mom/dad/grandma!" They'll love it!

Let's Put on a Show!

Wow, starlets! The moment has arrived—
it's finally your chance to be a star. You've practiced all week,
you're all dressed up, and now you're ready to go! Just make
sure that you've got the setting right—then let's do it, girls!

Don't worry if you don't have a real stage—an open area at one end of a room with enough space for you to sing, dance, or act in will be fine. You don't even have to appear from behind a curtain. Just make sure that there's a gap between the stage and the seating area. You can appear through a doorway at the back or side of the room and walk to the stage—or you can dance your way to it!

Lighting is important because it creates the right atmosphere. Try and make sure that any curtains are closed and, if you don't have a spotlight, get your friends to hold flashlights and shine them on you for easy, perfect spotlights!

Use the star stencil to make lots of stars. Cover them in glitter or tinfoil and stick them all over the room and on curtains and doors.

Okay, it's almost your turn. Are you nervous? So are we! But don't worry—just remember to breathe slowly, relax those shoulders, and keep your arms loosely by your sides. Now take a deep breath and go for it!

Don't panic if you make a mistake—just keep going, and no one will notice that you've forgotten the words or missed a step in your routine.

Oh, and afterward don't forget to take a bow. Just bend forward from your waist and keep smiling. We don't think that we need to tell you how to sign an autograph—we bet you've practiced a thousand times, right?

Phew! We did it!

Pause For Applause . . .

It's been one week, and we've made our dreams come true!
We were *soooo* nervous, but now it's all over—and guess what?
The Rising Stars are all real stars. Hooray! But remember, you
have to keep up the hard work. A true star shines all the time—
not just when she's performing.

Now that we're a huge success, we've discovered that
you have to be prepared for fame and fortune. It's a lot
of hard work. If you're going to be the best, you have
to prepare a speech to say when you win awards.
Remember, you should mention all the people who
helped you along the way. Not just us, silly—your mom
and dad, too. And never forget to thank your fans—who
knows, some of them could be stars-in-training as well!

We have a few people to thank . . .

We've taught you how to be a star, but it's up to you to follow the rules. That way, fame, fortune, and success will be yours for as long as you want—and who could complain about that? Right, girls?

Rising Star Rules

1. Have confidence in yourself.
2. Practice, practice, practice!
3. Exercise that body!
4. Eat healthily–shine inside and out.
5. Do your homework. Find out all you can about your favorite stars.
6. Always wear your sunglasses.
7. Ask your friends for advice–and listen to it!
8. Don't be afraid to make your dreams come true.
9. Don't forget to breathe!
10. Always remember that you're a STAR!

Scarlett x   Kelly x   Danielle x

Miss Danielle's Dressing Room

Thanks for letting us share our star secrets with you. We've had a great time. Now we have our star certificates, just like you! Bye—and keep shining!